SNAPPED BY SAM!

Level 5A

Written by Melanie Hamm
Illustrated by Emmeline Pidgen
Reading Consultant: Betty Franchi

About Phonics

Spoken English uses more than 40 speech sounds. Each sound is called a *phoneme*. Some phonemes relate to a single letter (d-o-g) and others to combinations of letters (sh-ar-p). When a phoneme is written down, it is called a *grapheme*. Teaching these sounds, matching them to their written form, and sounding out words for reading is the basis of phonics.

Early phonics instruction gives children the tools to sound out, blend, and say the words without having to rely on memory or guesswork. This instruction gives children the confidence and ability to read unfamiliar words, helping them progress toward independent reading.

About the Consultant

Betty Franchi is an American educator with a Bachelor's Degree in Elementary and Middle Education as well as a Master's Degree in Special Education. Betty holds a National Boards for Professional Teaching Standards certification. Throughout her 24 years as a teacher, she has studied and developed an expertise in Phonetic Awareness and has implemented phonetic strategies, teaching many young children to read, including students with special needs.

Reading tips

This book focuses on the *t* sound
(made with the letters *ed*) as in tripp**ed**.

Tricky and/or new words in this book

Any words in bold may have unusual spellings
or are new and have not yet been introduced.

> **Tricky and/or new words in this book**
>
> ### fence picture

Extra ways to have fun with this book

After the readers have finished the story, ask them
questions about what they have just read.

What things did Sam snap that annoyed his friends?
Why did Sam step on the fence?

What would
you snap?

A Pronunciation Guide

This grid contains the sounds used in the stories in levels 4, 5, and 6 and a guide on how to say them.

/ă/ as in pat	/ā/ as in pay	/âr/ as in care	/ä/ as in father
/b/ as in bib	/ch/ as in church	/d/ as in deed/ milled	/ĕ/ as in pet
/ē/ as in bee	/f/ as in fife/ phase/ rough	/g/ as in gag	/h/ as in hat
/hw/ as in which	/ĭ/ as in pit	/ī/ as in pie/ by	/îr/ as in pier
/j/ as in judge	/k/ as in kick/ cat/ pique	/l/ as in lid/ needle (nēd'l)	/m/ as in mom
/n/ as in no/ sudden (sŭd'n)	/ng/ as in thing	/ŏ/ as in pot	/ō/ as in toe
/ô/ as in caught/ paw/ for/ horrid/ hoarse	/oi/ as in noise	/ʊ/ as in took	/ū/ as in cute

/ou/ as in **ou**t	/p/ as in **p**op	/r/ as in **r**oar	/s/ as in **s**au**ce**
/sh/ as in **sh**ip/ di**sh**	/t/ as in **t**igh**t**/ stopp**ed**	/th/ as in **th**in	/th/ as in **th**is
/ŭ/ as in c**u**t	/ûr/ as in **ur**ge/ t**er**m/ f**ir**m/ w**or**d/ h**ear**d	/v/ as in **v**al**ve**	/w/ as in **w**ith
/y/ as in **y**es	/z/ as in **z**ebra/ **x**ylem	/zh/ as in vi**s**ion/ plea**s**ure/ gara**ge**/	/ə/ as in **a**bout/ it**e**m/ edibl**e**/ gall**o**p/ circ**u**s
/ər/ as in butt**er**			

Be careful not to add an /uh/ sound to /s/, /t/, /p/, /c/, /h/, /r/, /m/, /d/, /g/, /l/, /f/ and /b/. For example, say /fff/ not /fuh/ and /sss/ not /suh/.

Sam had a new camera.
He snapped pictures
of everything he saw.

He snapped the birds as
they flapped and the dogs
as they yapped.

Sam snapped Sally as she skipped.
She did not mind.

He snapped Chaz as he shopped.
He did not mind.

Sam snapped Ben as he tripped.
Ben was fed up.

Sam snapped Jo as she slipped.
Jo was angry.

Sam snapped Billy as he
flopped and napped.

Billy woke and was cross.

Sam saw a horse as it
clip-clopped down the lane.

He stepped on the **fence** to get near but he slipped off.

Sam dropped into a hole.
He was trapped.

Ben, Jo, and Billy stopped by.
Were they still cross?

No, they were not cross. They threw
Sam a rope and he gripped it.

They helped him up from the hole.

Sam was saved and Jo clapped.

Up popped Tim. He snapped
the rescue with his camera.

Ben, Jo, Billy, and Sam
looked at the **picture**.

It was good! Now Sam just
snaps if everybody is happy.

OVER 48 TITLES IN SIX LEVELS
Betty Franchi recommends...

Other titles to enjoy from Level 4

The Maze	Fairy Fay's Bad Day	Eve the Knight
978 1 84898 771 5	978 1 84898 772 2	978 1 84898 773 9

Some titles from Level 5

Max's Trip	George the Genius Gerbil	Budge Troll, Budge!
978 1 84898 776 0	978 1 84898 777 7	978 1 84898 778 4

Some titles from Level 6

What Wally Wanted	Superhero Ed!	The Robot Bop
978 1 84898 779 1	978 1 84898 780 7	978 1 84898 782 1

An Hachette Company
First Published in the United States by TickTock, an imprint of Octopus Publishing Group.
www.octopusbooksusa.com

Copyright © Octopus Publishing Group Ltd 2013

Distributed in the US by
Hachette Book Group USA
237 Park Avenue, New York NY 10017, USA

Distributed in Canada by
Canadian Manda Group
165 Dufferin Street, Toronto, Ontario, Canada M6K 3H6

ISBN 978 1 84898 775 3

Printed and bound in China
10 9 8 7 6 5 4 3 2 1